30 Days-Streams of Consciousness
Book 3
Fire and Ice: A Love Story
Lucinda Moebius

30 Days-Streams of Consciousness Book 3
Fire and Ice: A Love Story
Copyright ©2016 by L.E. Moebius

Haven Novels 2011
Haven Novels
www.mywritersplace.com
First Hardcover Edition: 2016
First Paperback Edition: 2016
First E-Book Edition: 2016

30 Days-Streams of Consciousness:
Fire and Ice: A Love Story
a novella by L.E. Moebius. -1st. ed. p.cm.
ISBN-13: 9780692730195
Cover design (Picture and Lettering)
by Jamin Mattison
Printed in the United States of America
Haven Novels

Introduction

Stream of consciousness refers to the practice of writing down ideas as they come into your head. The conventions of grammar and appropriateness of language is usually ignored when using this literary technique. For those of you who cringe at the misplaced metaphor, or the comma splice, or the occasionally correctly spelled wrong word so frequently seen in this day of spell-check reliability, don't worry there are a lot more things in here to worry about. Concern yourself with the raw emotions expressed when two individuals are consumed, destroyed, reformed and recreated by love.

Match

I only saw you for a moment before you faded away. You were so beautiful I wanted to get closer and study every line, every angle. Do you even realize how beautiful you are? My passion flared and burned hot as I saw you pressed against the window. I tried to get closer, but I was afraid you would melt into the darkness.

Did you see me? I was there. I wanted you to notice me, but it all happened so fast. For a moment I burned my way into the darkness and made myself as big as I could just so you would see me. I wanted to be big and strong and beautiful so you would notice me and finally creep towards me, but I was so tiny in the night I doubt you even noticed me.

Can you love me? Oh, please! Say you can give yourself to me. Even if it is just for the brief moment of our existence. We both exist in such an insubstantial moment. I don't even know if what I saw was real.

Next time I will not fade away so fast. I will find a way to stay and see you in all of your glory. So beautiful. So fragile.

Did you see me? Did you want me, too?

I promise you, next time I will stay longer. Please, do not go away so quickly.

You blossomed like flowers all glistening with light and love. I wish I could have reached out to you, but the coldness of the night danced across me and forced me away. I will look for you tonight. I will move as close to the window as I dare and watch and wait.

Will you come to me tonight?

I will live again when the moment is right. Look for me, as I will look for you. Let me caress you and warm you in the night. I will leave traces of my warmth against you until you melt into me and we become one.

Frost

I saw you. At least I think I did. You flashed bright in the night, but then you were gone. I wanted to see more and I tried to reach out to you, but I was surrounded by my own limitations.

I wonder if you saw me for what I was or if you only saw the show I put on for others. I felt so fake, made up to look like the fairies created me. Did you see the real me? I hope you could see past the fancy decoration and the sparkle and sensation I created.

Did you see the marks the others put on me? Fingertips brushing against me, warming me, melting me? I could feel the breath of children warming me in the night. They were there, surrounding me, touching me. I wanted to scream at them to let them know they were destroying me but I was frozen on place. You were the only hope I had. The only bright spot in a sea of darkness. Why didn't you come to me? Didn't you see how much I needed you?

When I see you again I hope you will come to me. Please, don't fade away again. I will wait for you in the night. Don't go away so quickly next time. I want to see you in your true form, bright and beautiful and flashing through the darkness.

I thought I was alone in the night. I didn't know there was anyone out there with the same longing as me. You burned through the night, bringing me the love I needed. Yes, I know we barely saw each other, but I know I love you. Your form, your light, your voice, your strength. I love every aspect of what you are just as I know you will love me.

Do you love me yet? Do you know what I can be for you? It is the moment, the flash, the burn I crave from you. It will not linger long, our love. It is not meant to last long. Some love is meant to last a moment and then burn out quickly. It will be enough to sustain us for a lifetime, this love of ours.

Lighter

I could burn longer if you needed me to, my love. There is so much more to me now. I know I stayed for just a moment, until their use for me was over, but there is much more substance to me now.

I was closer to you today. I could feel the coolness of your form as you swirled by me. I wanted to warm you and watch as your cold shape pooled into something more malleable. Could you change for me if I needed you to be something different or will you always be the cold, hard shape you were forced to become?

I want to change for you. I want to become something better, something more useful. I know I have my uses. They have forced me to become what they needed and now I have become tiny and insignificant. You could magnify me. You could make me something great again.

Will you change me? Will you teach me what it means to burn bright again? I caught a tiny glimpse of myself reflected back from your glance. A tiny fraction of what I could become under your guidance.

Do we need to change for one another? Can you accept me for what I am?

No. I know I need to change. It is the nature of our existence to want to become better. I am so much greater than the sum of my parts. Just look at me. What do you see? I am tiny and quiet and am barely formed, but when I am put to use I am unstoppable. From the tiny insignificance I burst forth and become something more powerful than even you could imagine.

Think about what we could be if we were together. What power and majesty could we create? I want to build the world with you. Can't you picture it? I will mold and form you and you will magnify me in my greatness.

We have power on our own. We are strong and beautiful and amazing and we can create great things. But, think about what we can do together. Do not float by me again, sitting there in your cold, shapeless glory. I will warm you and give you a form more magnificent than anyone could imagine.

Stop and see me, my love. Look into my being and find your soul.

Ice Cube

You burned so brightly against the darkness of the night. I longed to reach out for you but I was dawn away into the crowd. Everyone needs me more than I need myself and I can't find a way to get to you. I want you. I need you. I know you will magnify me in all of my magnificence.

When will I see you again? Do not let me lose myself again.

You can rescue me. Please. I have lost myself and I don't know what to do.

I am desperate.

I am afraid.

I am alone.

I am contained in the darkness and they won't let me out.

Find me.

You are the only one who has the power to find me in the dark.

I am forced to keep myself small.

I am shrinking every day.

Soon I will be insignificant.

I don't mean to be so hard and cold.

I can soften my hard edges for you.

If only you come and find me.

Cigarette

I needed space. I didn't want you to see my dark side. Why did you have to follow me? There is so much ugliness in me when I am like this and I didn't want you to know about it yet.

Maybe it's because I was trying to hide my own ugliness, but I never knew you had a dark side too. I didn't mean to hurt you. I should have never called you ugly or dirty. Please, I knew you were beautiful once and you could be beautiful again.

I saw the tears streaming away as you melted into your pain. I wanted to gather it up and give it back to you. It looked so painful, the rivulets streaming away from your body and taking away from your greatness.

Why do we have to show our ugly side so soon? I wish I could find a way to replace what you have lost, but once the damage has been caused the scars will always show.

I burned away my light and dropped ashes all through your loveliness. I burned into your soul until there was no danger of you ever remaining the same. Can you ever see me the same way again? Can you ever find me beautiful and charming and strong? Can you like what I created?

The worst part of all of this is I did this to myself. It was my own weakness, my own addiction washing over me causing all this damage.

I want to promise I will never hurt you again, but I know I am weak. There is no promise I can make when my own weakness overshadows my ability to overcome my addiction.

You could be my new addiction. Let me make you my habit. Teach me to be strong and compassionate. Let me see the pain I caused so I can see what I need to do to be strong.

Please forgive me so I can forgive myself.

Slush

You weren't supposed to see my ugly side. I tried to hide it from you, but you plowed your way through me and found me hidden away in the corner. I was covered over with grey and filth and I couldn't shrink away from you fast enough.

I can't believe you still want me even after I showed you all of my ugliness. How can you find beauty even through all of this?

You were ugly and hateful. I could see the filth rolling off of you and yet I still wanted you. I know what danger you cause and still I wanted you. Can you still want me, too?

How can we move past this moment? There is only so much hurt a body can take before it is done. Maybe I need to stay here and lick my wounds until I can make myself strong again.

The more I give away the further I shrink into the corner. This is the first time I have done anything for myself since we began this dance.

Give me some time. I promise I will come back beautiful and whole and strong. This was just one moment of weakness. It was not the real me.

Candle

I'm not any bigger than I was last time you saw me, but I burned ever so much longer for you. I could see myself reflected a thousand times in your smoothness. You magnify my brilliance a thousand times brighter than I could ever reflect myself. We were so close I could almost touch you, but I knew if I reached out and caressed you I wouldn't be able to survive.

Is this where we are? Longing to be near each other and yet unable to coexist. I can feel your cold breath brushing against me, causing my life-force to flutter with every exhalation. Why do we have to wait so long to be together?

We have come so far you and I. I thought I lost you for a moment when we saw each other in our weakness, but the moment passed and we survived. Don't you see how much more strong and beautiful our love is now? Please forgive me for all the pain I caused. I will not survive much longer if I cannot have you.

You are shrinking away with every moment. Please do not pull yourself away from me. I will stay here, where I am safe and wait for you to decide if reaching out to me.

You have forced yourself into a shape others will find beautiful, but if one thing goes wrong, one crack appears in the form, the image you give to the world will crumble and fall. I can see the beauty in the form under the shape. Why do you hide your true beauty underneath the outer shell? I can see the true you and I don't understand how you think these outer trappings make you more beautiful. I can see myself reflected deep within your soul and I find I am beautiful only when I am magnified from within you.

Can you feel my love for you? It is the only thing keeping me whole. Without it I will be made small and insignificant again. Thank you for your beauty and your strength. It is what makes me whole.

Ice Sculpture

I wanted to show you all of the beauty I could possess after the ugliness you found in me last time. I hate being ugly. I hate that you saw me in all of my ugliness. Maybe in my zeal to be remarkable I forced myself into a shape you no longer found beautiful.

I took in every ounce of your light and reflected it back to you so you could find your own beauty. Every inch of me was devoted to highlighting the beauty surrounding me.

Did you see me? I made myself large for you. Every inch of my form was carved, smoothed and polished just so I could reflect your beauty. You were lovely in my glow.

I tried to push myself through the crowds, but the warmth overwhelmed me and I needed to withdraw to the place where I felt safe. Every moment I felt my beauty melting away. Hands brushed against me finding out my most sacred secrets, filling me with doubt and dread. But, even with all the damage they still couldn't discover all my secrets and I was able to find your beauty.

There is more to me than what you see on the outside. I have light and beauty and strength all wrapped up in the lines and edges of my outer form. I am not nearly as polished as I appear to be. What do you really know about me? I am hidden within the outer form. I know you saw it. I could see it in your form as I reflected your image back to you.

I want to feel your gentle caress against me. Do not fear me. I am not afraid of you. I know you would never hurt me, at least not deliberately. Your light allows me to fulfill my purpose.

Can I be beautiful without you? Yes. I know I have function and beauty and purpose in this life. I am beautiful, even without your approval. I don't need you, I want you. Isn't that the difference?

Pilot Light

I waited for you in the darkness, hiding myself until I could see you again. No, I wasn't trying to stalk you or hide myself as you slowly brought yourself forward. I wasn't watching or waiting, I was just resting while waiting for you. I didn't want to show myself to the world because I wanted to belong to you and only you.

I watched you in your silence as you put the world to sleep and softened the hard corners of my life. You were silent and cold and beautiful in the light and I fell even more in love with you.

Waiting for you in the darkness was the best part of my life. I made myself small to hide away from pain and sorrow, but you found me in my quiet places where I was sure I was safe. I am no longer hidden and alone. There are no more dark and quiet places. I need to show myself to the world so the world can see the beauty you created for them.

I will flare up and shine brightly so we can see what you have created for them. There is no beauty in the world without light to see. I am saving you for the world to see. There is strength and beauty in my light as I shower you with brightness. Can you see what I have to offer? I will stay here, steady and quiet, until you need me again. Then I will flare to life and show you how beautiful you are.

I am so glad you decided to show me the real you. The soft, gentle side of what you can be. Don't ever try to force yourself into a false form again. You are more than beautiful enough in your natural form.

I promise not to hide myself for very long. Do you see? The only way I can remain hidden is if I am in perfect control of everything. If I am in chaos I will become harmful and sorrow will follow me for the rest of my days. I will control myself for you and only you. Without you I am nothing and everything and I will be the destroyer of all things. Hold yourself in place so I can find my self-control.

Snow

You made me find myself. I have found my true form because of you. Your touch has blessed my very life and made me free. I needed your strength to see what I could truly become.

I am blessed by your very existence. Every breath you take makes me more complete. I am soft and barely formed, but this is the true me. Do you see how I sparkle as I drift through the light? Every curve is designed to bring me closer to you. I can find you, even in your hidden, secret places.

I have no desire to hide myself away from you. Why do you need to hide yourself from me? There is nothing you need to fear. I know I look unsubstantial and transient, but I have no intention of going anywhere any time soon. I will be here for a long time. Do not hide your strength and beauty away from me. Yes, even while you burn away your pain I see your beauty.

I have made the world quiet and peaceful just so I can find you in the silence. I will flitter around you and dance in your glow until we are both too exhausted to move.

I love you. Is it too soon to say the words? I don't think it's too soon, but I'm so fresh and new at this I don't know if I'm doing the right thing. Is this how I'm supposed to act when I'm in love? I've never felt this way before so I wouldn't know. Tell me what I'm supposed to do. Show me how I'm supposed to act. I will be here in the quiet, waiting.

Fireplace

This moment. This is all I need. We can live forever in this moment. I heard your whispers as you slipped through my consciousness in the night. Every moment I breathe through you and can feel your caress. Even when you're gone I can still feel you against me.

This is perfection. Every breath, every flash, every touch means I can be closer to you. I want to feel you against me again and again. We can sit here in the darkness until we are full of warmth and light and hope. This is our life. This is our moment.

Your breath soothes my pain and puts aside my fears. There is no life without you. There is no hope without you. Can you find your own peace with me?

Come, bask in my warmth. Show me how you can live through my light. The beauty I see in you reflects my glory and love. You are beautiful, even without me, but my strength magnifies everything you have to offer.

I will offer you everything I have. Do you see? I can offer you my strength, my love, everything in this world and beyond. This world is more than I can offer, but I will give it to you anyway.

I am not afraid. You are with me. We will face the storm together. You will hold back the winds and change and I will warm the home front. This is what we can be together. I know you can feel how we can rule the world. Or at least we can hold our little corner safe against the best they can throw at us.

I will no longer hide. I am here for every moment of your life as you are here for me. I have put all of my trust in you. My love. My world. This is the rest of our days, together. We are each other's hope. We are each other's dreams. We are each other.

Icicles

I'm building a fortress here. It's going to take time and patience, but if you wait for me you will find beauty in my strength. Every inch of life I give builds the walls we need to be safe. This is pain for me, nothing but pain as I build my strength to fight the storm. Every inch of pain is worth it if it will keep you safe.

I will revel in your warmth and light. Every moment with you is magnified a hundred times. When your strength fades I will be there to support and care for you.

I created this form for you. It is not forced or dark. It is what I was born to be. Thank you for showing me my true beauty. I can grow into my own strength only if you are with me. This is what I always wanted to be. I can feel my pulse throbbing through every inch of my existence. Oh, beautiful life! You are for me!

You breathe life into me every day. Without you I would be trapped in my false form, living my life only to reflect the beauty of others. I would never have known what beauty I could give the world.

The storm is raging, inside and out. Do you feel it? No, I didn't think you could. I am keeping the storm out just so I can keep you safe forever. Without you there is no me. I know you don't believe me, but you are the reason for my existence. Can you hear the wind rolling through the trees? Its rumbling across the tiles of the roof, forcing its way through the cracks of the doors and the windows, pushing against the shelter. I will not let it pass. The storm can rage against the walls, but it will never get through me. I will tear myself in two, or three, or four, just to keep you safe in the night.

The cool air caresses me until, inch by inch, I become larger and stronger. I know, right now, I look so tiny and fragile, but this is just the beginning of my rebirth. Soon I will rule the world and with you by my side we will conquer every corner and cover every inch of the Earth with our power.

Torch

This is the best we have ever been. The best we will ever be. We have survived the storm and emerged unscathed. This has been the test and we have passed. My joy fills me and makes me brighter and stronger than ever. Oh my love, my joy, my peace. You have given me more than I could ever hope for in this life and the next.

Come, join me in the glory of this moment. We have joy in the morning and satisfaction in the night. My love, my joy, my peace. I will carry you through the brightness of my days. Your true form shines through every aspect of your being. I never imagined you could be so glorious. Allow me to come closer so I can gaze upon your loveliness.

You have given up the trappings of the world and allowed your true form the freedom to exist. I can see the light of the world reflected in you. Nothing could be more glorious or beautiful. There is splendor in the natural aspects of the world.

Allow me to light the way. I will be the light on your life, a guide to your path. The journey will be long, but together we will find ourselves.

Are you happy? Can you find joy in the tiny things, the moments of peace and calm? I can't promise there will be no more storms. I can't promise a smooth path free of all obstacles. All I can promise is to continue to light the way.

Will you join me on this journey? Sometimes, when the path is simple, we are lulled into the falseness of going the easy way and then we lose ourselves. I know the path is strange and hard to see, but I will be your guide. My joy will be your joy. My strength will be your strength.

The path will be long and the journey hard, but at the end we will be stronger and brighter. Join me so we may find joy.

Frozen Puddle

Loving you is so easy. I almost forgot everything you had to offer, until I saw you in this moment. Your strength overwhelmed me for a moment and I was blinded by your glory.

What just happened? I almost lost myself in the light and life you gave me. We survived the storm together, but now the night is dark and I am afraid. Light the path before me so I can find my way. Be the guide to my feet and the strength for my soul.

Can I lean on you? I am so weak I know I will not be able to find my way alone. I am spread thin and my surface is broken. I am forced to huddle here on the cold, hard ground and my fear overwhelms me. You are strong. In you I will reform myself.

I can depend on no other. I have been trodden upon and broken into tiny pieces and I don't think I can take any more. Please, pick me up. Support me. Love me. I don't know if I can take this anymore.

The storm has broken me. It has left me scattered and alone. You are my only hope. My only support. Pick me up, piece me back together. Give me back my life.

I will be reformed by you. I do not need to be changed or fixed or recreated. I just need to be made back to what I was before. You have seen me in all my true forms. You know what I should be, instead of this, what I am now.

Bring me back to my beautiful glory. Find what I should be and force me back into that shape. I can be what I was before. This doesn't have to change me. This doesn't have to change us. Give me hope. Give me a chance. Give us hope. Give us a chance.

The path is dark. Light the way. I will follow. I may take longer and I may stumble until I get my bearings, but I will find my way back to you. The storm is over and you will light my way.

Spontaneous Combustion

How can just existing cause so much pain? Every inch of me is flaring up in pain and anguish. There is nothing I can do to stop this burning. You are my love, my soul, my life and you sit there watching me destroy myself. Is there nothing you can do for me? Is there nothing you can say?

I never knew there could be so much pain in the cold. You looked warm. You caste off the shackles of what you were and became something stronger and more powerful than even I could imagine. Yet, you sit there in your perfected state, unfeeling, uncaring, unaware. Is there nothing more I can do to assuage your pain?

There is hope in your aspect, but you are fading fast. Everything about your appearance seems so substantial, but even as you freeze me with your looks you are disappearing into the mists as if you never even existed.

I want to embrace you, pull you close, hold you. But, I am afraid of the pain. Is there nothing more for us? Why does everything have to flash through so fast and then fade away?

I burn so bright in just this moment. It is building up inside of me and there is nothing I can do to control it. Can you feel it? I want it to stop hurting, even if it is just for a moment. I want the pain and ache and sorrow to just fade away. I want that moment of peace denied from me for so long. Don't you want it, too? Can't you see what we can be if we just take a moment to stop and breathe?

I know you are hurting, too. I know the pain is eating away at you and you want it to burn away your edges and your sorrow. We can get through this moment. I know there is hope for us.

Do not fade away into the darkness. Stay with me at least for a little while.

Dry Ice

I am nothing. I am hollow. I am as insubstantial as the air you breathe. I am even less than that because I cannot breathe life into a soul. Is there more you need from me? Is there any more I can do that hasn't already been done.

There is pain in every inch of my soul and I am the one who caused it to be there. You say I am cold. You say I burn. I am trying to build a shield around the pain so I don't feel any more.

It is so cold I burn. Every inch of me is on fire and I want to throw everything away. There will be no sign of my existence. Everything will be burned away in the final cleansing.

I am cold and hard because I have to do what I can to protect myself from pain. I am cold and hard because there is no one else left to trust except myself. I am cold and hard because this is the way I was formed by the circumstances of my life. I am cold and hard because this is the way I need to be.

You could never understand. You stand there, a pillar, a burning desire, a never fading light, and mock the suffering I have endured. All you see is the end result. You don't see the crucible designed to burn away the impurities and create the final form. This is ugly to you; this creature I have become. I know, I see it reflected in your entire aspect.

I am nothing more than insubstantial smoke given the form of life. You can see it as I become smaller and smaller and inconsequential. As you flash into existence and fade away into nothingness you will begin to understand. There is no need to explain this to you anymore. You wouldn't understand anyway.

House Fire

How could you betray me this way? I trusted you. I gave you my heart, my love, my life and you have torn me down and shattered me! God, I have never felt this kind of pain before. You have stabbed me through all my sacred places and shattered my soul. Can't you see the pain you are causing me? Every inch of me is shattered and broken.

There can be no trust, no faith, no love in this. Do not try to persuade me you were thinking of me. How is this supposed to help me? All of this is nothing but pain. It started out so small and innocent, hidden where no one could see. But now, this is raging through everything I hold sacred. How can I offer protection when I can't even protect myself?

You did this to me. you were supposed to protect me, not tear me down to my roots and leave me hollow. I am shattered and torn down to my foundation. There is nothing left for me to save.

No! You cannot come in to what is left. There is nothing here for you. I will sit here quietly and gather up the pieces you have scattered and see if there is anything worth salvation. You do not need to be here for this. There is nothing here for you.

Do you find this enjoyable? Do you revel in my pain? The only reason you are here is so you can see my pain.

Yes, I know you are there. You cannot remain hidden forever. I know your secrets and I know how you hide yourself. You can't hide your true self any more. I know the darkest parts of your soul and I am not afraid.

Your betrayal will never be forgotten. How can I forgive this level of destruction? There is nothing left. Nothing to say. Nothing to save.

Black Ice

I did not cause this. You brought this on yourself. You dare blame me for your destruction? Can you not take responsibility for your own actions? I did nothing to destroy you.

This is you, it's not me. I will go find my own way. My path will be hidden and sacred and you will not see me until I decide. I'm still here, hidden in plain sight. I'm not going to show myself until I know I am safe. You destroyed the world and expect me to take the blame.

I have my own faults. I don't need to take the blame for what you do, too. Every inch of this path is strewn with my faults. I'm not afraid of the trail of destruction I leave behind. I earned every mark, every scar, every bump creating this unique shape. I don't blame anyone else for what created me. you need to take responsibility for your own form. Your own shape.

I have no more faith in you, but I did this to myself, too. I opened myself to your advances and allowed you into my sacred places. I feel the pain of the burn you caused, but I know when I rebuild myself I will be stronger and better than ever before.

I know you can't see me. You can't see anything beyond yourself. All you want to do is trod on me. There is nothing you can do to fix this.

I'm done.

Campfire

I needed to confine myself to this tiny little circle in order to build myself up again. I can't let you in yet. I don't trust you. This is going to take time. I don't know if it can be fixed. I don't know if I want to fix it.

I don't like you very much. I love you more than I have loved anyone else before, but I don't like you very much right now. I guess I'm going to have to love you until I like you again. Maybe this is what being in love is all about. I can see every flaw in your surface and yet I still want you to be a part of me.

Why did this have to happen to us? I don't understand how love can be so strong and still leave me so bereft of hope.

I want to hate you. You don't even know how much I want to rip out my heart and leave it on the side of the road so there is no more reason to give you all of my hope.

I know this is as much my fault as it is yours. I take responsibility for my part of everything. It takes two to fight and I made sure to play my part, maybe too well.

Let me sit here, in my tiny little circle, licking my wounds and thinking about how I can remake myself. No, I still love you. That is part of the problem. Even if I allowed myself to be destroyed I would still love you. You are the world and I am just a small part of it.

Hail

I want to lash at you and pound into your body until you acknowledge me. You know I'm here, you need to at least tell me you feel me. I'm reaching out here. I know this is painful, but right now this is all I have.

I'm trying. I really am. I don't want to hurt you anymore. Maybe I'll leave. I don't want to go, but I will if you want me gone. I do love you. I miss your warmth and brilliance. Let me stay here by your side for just a few more minutes.

I am not trying to force away your warmth. Can you not see me leaning into you, curling up next to you, reaching out to you, trying to pull you close? Please, bring your warmth closer.

There is hope for us, yet. I know you love me. I can see the desire in your form. Can we forget the past and move into the future, or has the flame faded? What do we have left?

Give me some hope. Just a little glimpse into your light. I am sorry for all the pain I've caused. I know I have caused you more pain than you have ever experienced before. All my hopes and dreams were tied up in you. You betrayed me as much as I betrayed you.

Your beauty and strength are reaching into my soul and giving me strength. The storm is over. All of the pain is gone in a flash. I know what we have will never be the same. This will leave scars. I like scars. I know it sounds strange, but scars are badges of honor. They aren't ugly. Scars just mean you've been through something tough and came out the other end whole.

I'm whole now. All my holes are plugged up and I won't leak all over the place now.

I miss you. Please, let me rest here and gather in your warmth.

Embers

Move over. You're hogging all the warmth. Ah, yes. That's perfect. It's so comfortable here buy your side. So peaceful. So quiet. I love to look at you in this peaceful state.

The air is so fresh and clean here. Can you feel it? It's like the world has cleaned itself of all impurities and giving us a chance to start over. I'll stay here, in this quiet little state, until you decide it has been long enough. Am I sharing enough with you? I don't want you to be alone and afraid.

I look at you and I know you have secrets beneath your surface. I can see the light reflected from your depths and I know there is life there. If I get to close will you crack under my weight and open up your depths? You would extinguish my light if I allowed myself to be swallowed up. In some ways I think it would be worth it. I wonder what it would be like to lose myself in your cool depths.

No, don't be afraid. I won't allow myself to be lost again. I am too strong for that. I found myself with you and then lost myself again, but now I have found myself without you and know what I am and what I can do.

The world has been made quiet and pure and you have shown me things can be beautiful again.

I think I understand love a little better now. Love isn't always patient and kind and sometimes it is full of anger and hate, but most importantly love can be found again, even if love has hurt.

You are the joy in my morning and my peace at night, but sometimes you cause my soul to become weary and I need to find rest. This moment is good. I am warm and safe and you are with me. We need to gather these moments close and gather them into our hearts to keep us warm and strong when the hard times come.

My beautiful peace. I will keep you warm through the night. Sleep well and when the morning comes we will find our way together.

Frozen Lake

I'm so thankful you are allowing me to stay here by your side. Your warmth is reaching into me, flooding my heart with strength. This is the best place in the world to be. I wouldn't want to be anywhere else. Let me curl into your warmth and nestle into your existence.

I have soothed the savage beast and have calmed the waters to give us a safe place to put our feet. You need to learn to trust me again. There is promise in the quiet. Like we are waiting for the good to come around again.

See, I knew we could find a way to be together again. Love doesn't conquer everything, but it is enough to sustain us until we can trust again.

We all have secrets buried beneath our surfaces. You are so quiet in your contemplations. What are you thinking about right now? Are you cold and afraid or are you like me, just enjoying the beauty of this night?

I will be here, by your side, where I am meant to be. It will take time to mend the broken pieces of our trust, but what we will have at the end will be worth it.

I can feel the peace of the night washing over us, making everything new and fresh and clean. Thank you for this moment. Tonight it is just us and we have found our peace.

Sparks

I can only hope to dream to become what I was before. I can send out tiny pieces of myself into the darkness in the hopes I will become something great again. I allowed myself to be contained, to be controlled, to become small. My desire to be strong and big is overwhelming my sensibilities.

You will be with me as I grow again, as I become what I was before. Can I ever be returned to my former greatness? I need to find beauty in what I am now in order to find joy in what I can become.

I see you in your peaceful, glorious state. Waiting day by day for some great thing to happen. Life doesn't happen while we are sitting still. Life happens because we move, when we take chances, when we dare to breathe.

Every exhalation breathes more life into me. Do not begrudge me my need to grow just because I want to be different. I want to break out of this circle that constrains me. I want to explode.

I will join you as darkness comes to light your way and brighten the night. I will stay by your side until there is no more fear and you find your quiet heart beating in the stillness. My beacon will show you the path of change and when the morning comes we will be great again.

Ice Caps

The quiet pierces the night and eases into my soul. This is where I need to be right now. This is where I belong.

Do we belong together? I don't know, but I do know I am glad you are here, by my side.

I have found my quiet place. This is where I am most at peace. I will sit here, in the quiet, watching the world as everything else rushes by.

You do not need to stay here, although I think I need you with me. if you are here by my side I will find myself again.

Shhh…the quiet buries me and I am at peace.

Smoldering

We need to take this slow. It's hard to start all over again when we ran ahead so fast in the beginning. There is so much fuel ready to flare up again and we need to keep everything under control. I cannot lose you again, my love.

We will settle here for a time. Taking the opportunity to get to know each other once again. Let me discover the part of you that you have been keeping beneath the surface. I can see just a partial glimpse into your soul, but I know there is so much there for me to see.

I will dwell here, hidden from sight, waiting for the right time to declare myself again. There is more hope in these quiet places than there ever was in the expanse of the bright universe.

The quiet is seeping into my soul and I am finding myself in the darkness. I will wait and watch for your approach. I am not afraid of all the secrets you are bringing. There is no night so dark that I can't find the light reflected in myself.

The quiet rushes over me and I feel the darkness creeping ever closer. I don't think I have ever been in the dark before. I am glad you are beside me, even though you are mostly hidden from my sight. Come closer, I am not afraid.

Ice Burgs

I have shared with you everything except the secret parts of my most sacred soul. Are you afraid of me yet? Do you know what is hidden beneath the surface of my heart? There is more to fear than you could even imagine. Why have you not run away yet?

Are you truly willing to stay, even though there is things here you should truly fear? I have laid waste to the world, sank the sturdiest of ships and changed the course of tides, and yet you still stay there, waiting. What is it you see in me to find this journey worth the fight?

Is there hope in love? I think if you stay I might get used to you and then we will never be able to part. I have done my best to put you aside, to extinguish the love I feel for you, but I cannot stop my heart from needing you near me.

I can turn and reveal to you the secrets I have buried beneath the surface. Is that enough to cause you to run? If you see the secrets I have hidden will you hide your light from my hope and heart?

You say you are not afraid. You say your love for me will always be strong. Perhaps I will believe you this time.

I will give this love a chance. You have burned so strong and still for the longest time. My love can never glow as strong as yours. I can only reflect back that which you give me. But, in that reflection I can magnify your light a hundred fold.

You will be my guiding light and I will be your mirror. Can there be anything more powerful than that.

When two souls are destined to collide and bring forth the destiny that has been foretold there is no force in the world that can prevent their joining as one. What will we create in our union? Will it have value for the world? My love will ever grow as we change into what we are destined to be.

Wild Fire

Finally, I am free. I can be who I was destined to be. You made this possible. Everything I have become is because you were there to help me find my true form. I am unconstrained, unbound!

I can feel the ecstasy of your love defining every inch of my existence. I can rage across the world, consuming all that gets in my way. In my wake the world will be reborn. I will cleanse the earth of iniquity and leave it to be reformed. You have shown me what purity is and helped me find my true purpose in the world.

We have nothing more to fear, the worst that could happen has come to pass. Every other moment in our life will be measured against this. There can be no greater pain or joy or love than what we have experienced in this moment.

You will always be beautiful to me. No matter what aspect you decide to show the world. I can see into your depths and see the purity deep within your soul. As I look into your stately depths I can't help but feel pride and joy and love.

I will purify this world so you have a place to rest your weary soul, my love. Every inch you carve into the surface as you push yourself forward and mark your place in the world gives me hope for our future. Nothing will prevent you from changing the world and I will be here, by your side changing it with you. We are opposite sides of the same coin. I will purify the world and you will give it form.

Ah, my love. We have shown the world what love should be. It can be more than just passion and pain. It is every aspect of emotion. I have burned with desire, smoldered in anger, raged with jealousy, flared up with passion, smoked out the truth, shone with an inner glow and showed you every aspect of my existence.

You have magnified my glory a million times and I have basked in the glow radiated from your aspect for eons. We will continue to grow and spread through this world, reforming it until there is nothing left to fear and we have made the world what we need it to be.

Glacier

This is our last bastion of glory. We will stand here, in the glory of what we have become and defend ourselves against everything the world can throw at us. I will take all the impurities of the world and bury them deep within the folds of my existence. I will grind down the edges of pain and force the world to conform to me.

We will confront the enemy together. You have sanctified the world and prepared the way for me to carve out the path I have determined for myself. We have created the perfect crucible together and have tested its powers.

You rage across the world and purify the path in moments while I sit here layered in quiet benisons of silent blessings slowly taking my affect upon time until, together, we have created a pure, quiet existence only we can understand.

I can see your glory reflected deep within my soul. I will preserve everything you create to be reformed and made new again. Deep within the womb of my form I will create a new life to be reborn into the world we have created.

This moment of love, this joining together, this power from within, is all we need to create the world in which we want to live.

Do not keep me at a distance. I am not a delicate, weak being meant to be put on display for the world to marvel at until I fade away. I have made myself strong enough to carry the weight of the world. There is nothing you can give me that I cannot take. Your power, your rage, your strength, your love. I can take every ounce of what you pile on me and reform it until it's ready to present to the world.

I will keep you safe. I will preserve your love until the world is ready to see as we are meant to be. Oh my love, we have held the secrets of the world within our hearts until it has grown too large to be contained. They world will never see us for what we can be unless we learn to carve a new existence into the surface of the earth and display what we can be.

You are strong and beautiful, raging through the world and purifying my existence. I will be here, waiting, as you move before me, preparing the way for me to create.

Steam

Do you see what we have become? Together we have created something new and beautiful and unafraid. This is what can happen when we allow love to be what it needs to be. There is no magic wand, no happiness for all of our lives, no eternity to exist only for each other. Love is not a spell to solve all of our problems. Love is what happens in the Ever After.

I used to believe in Fairy Tales, but now I know fairies don't exist. At least they don't exist for me. I do not need to wait for my Fairy Godmother to come and grant me a wish or turn me into a pumpkin (or something like that) in order to find love. Love is all around us, if we allow it to exist.

There are many faces of love and I have seen them all with you. I have felt passionate love as we embraced and created life. I have seen jealous love as we have torn ourselves apart and put ourselves back together. I have seen the quiet love that comes like the night, so subtly and without warning. I have seen the ugliness of love as it shows it's mirror companion of hate. And even in the quiet moments of hate, I know there is love waiting to be tempered, purified and reborn.

What is love, anyway? Can we really know what love is without knowing the sting of hate? Just wanting to love isn't enough to satisfy the souls craving for another being.

We weren't born to die, or to even live. We were born to love.

I can't make any more promises. Love is what I made it to be and nothing more. All I know is I am here, you are here and we have created something beautiful. We need to allow the beauty to find its own form and create its own moments of magic. We can read it fairy tales and give it our love story, but we can't save it from itself any more than our creators could save us from our own hearts and our own desires.

When our story is over they will look at us and say we were flawed. There was nothing there we haven't seen before. The story was just, meh. But, this was our story. We lived it. No one else could live it for us. From the outside our story was ugly. No one wants to see what is real. They want the magic, the fairy dust, the pumpkin.

Well, it's midnight and the ball is still going strong and there are others waiting for their turn to dance to the music. Let what we have created become its own destiny.

We are magical in our own lives and we have found our own Ever After.

About the Author

L. E. Moebius is a pseudonym for Lucinda Moebius. Lucinda has been a writer since she was a child and was first published in 2010. Since then she has worked hard to create unique visions and stories. Her work includes novels in multiple genres including: Science Fiction, Fantasy, Paranormal, Children's Books, Screenplays and Non-fiction. Lucinda has a Doctorate in Education and loves teaching, but her greatest desire is to help others understand how literature and writing can bring enlightenment and understanding to everyone. She offers book coaching and advice to everyone, whether they want it or not.

Website: www.mywritersplace.com

Other books by Haven Novels
Echoes of Savanna: Book One: The Parent Generation
http://www.amazon.com/gp/product/B006RM66QM

Raven's Song: Book One: T1 Generation
http://www.amazon.com/gp/product/B006YJ92GO

Write Well Publish Right
http://www.amazon.com/gp/product/1479316229

Feeder: Chronicles of the Soul Eaters Book 1
http://www.amazon.com/gp/product/0615968325

30 Days Stream of Consciousness V. 1
http://www.amazon.com/30-Days-Streams-Consciousness-1-ebook/dp/B01BW8JXBU

30 Days Streams of Consciousness Vol 2: A Haunting
http://www.amazon.com/30-Days-Stream-Consciousness-Haunting-ebook/dp/B01D7T9CFY

30 Days Streams of Consciousness Vol 3: Abduction
https://www.amazon.com/dp/B01D7T9CFY

www.ingramcontent.com/pod-product-compliance
Lightning Source LLC
Chambersburg PA
CBHW071215130626
46555CB00004B/1724